First published in 2022 by
Museums Victoria Publishing

11 Nicholson Street
Carlton, Victoria 3053, Australia

publications@museum.vic.gov.au

www.museumsvictoria.com.au

A catalogue record for this book is available from the National Library of Australia

ISBN 9781921833618

Design by Gemma Field

Proudly printed in Australia by Adams Print

This book draws inspiration from the *Gandel Gondwana Garden* at Melbourne Museum, which is generously supported by the Gandel Foundation.

1 3 5 7 9 10 8 6 4 2

Museums Victoria acknowledges the Wurundjeri and Boon Wurrung peoples of the Kulin Nations where we work, and First Peoples language groups and communities across Victoria and Australia. Our organisation, in partnership with the First Peoples of Victoria, is working to place First Peoples living cultures and histories at the core of our practice.

THE QUEST FOR KOOL

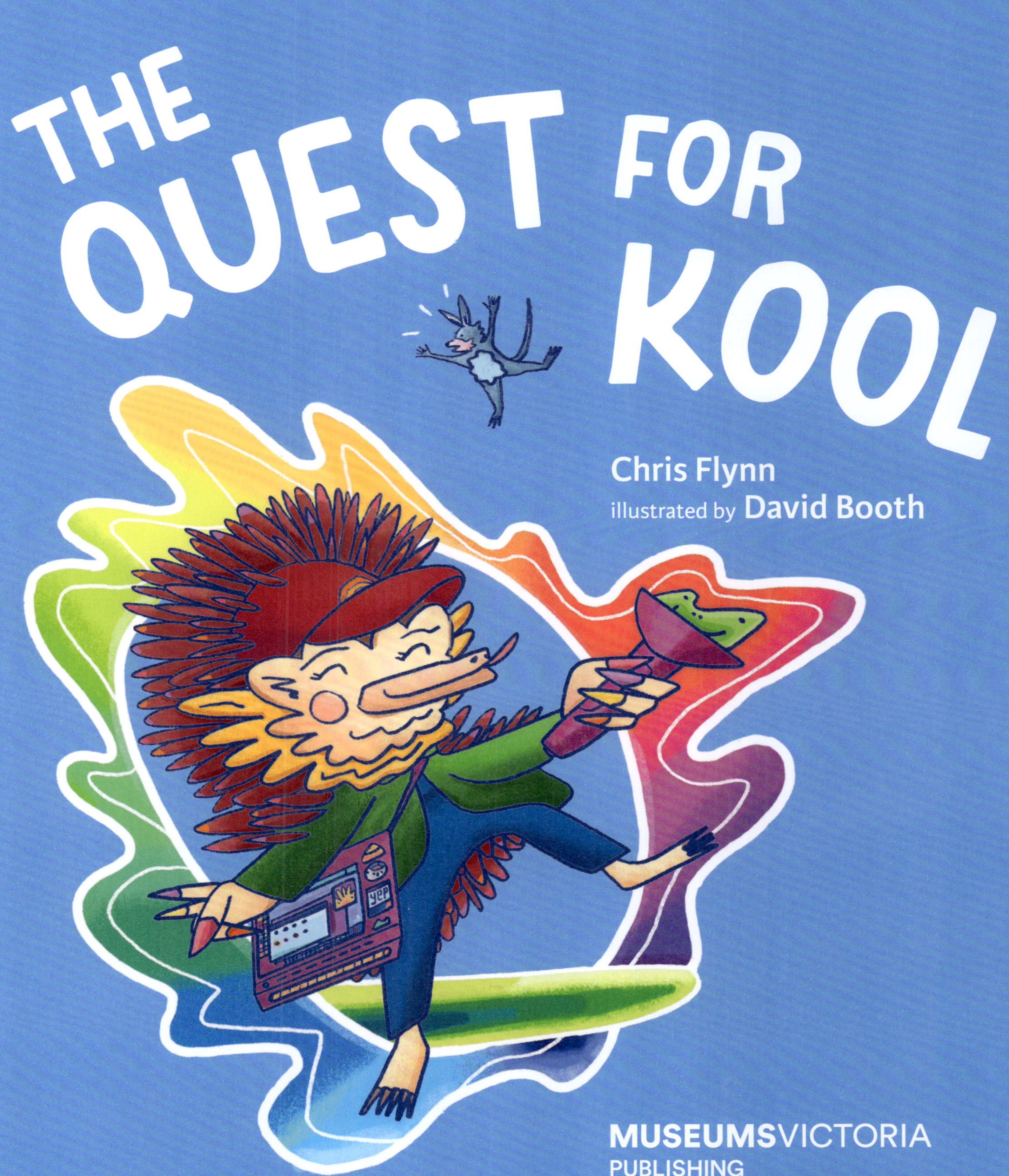

Chris Flynn

illustrated by **David Booth**

MUSEUMSVICTORIA
PUBLISHING

The museum's top researcher, Professor Kirrip, has been working tirelessly on a contraption that will help her travel through time and meet her all-time favourite animal: the long-extinct *Koolasuchus.*

Unfortunately, it doesn't work.

Kirrip takes a break to explore the museum garden. It's full of amazing plants and rocks, but she can't stop thinking about *Koolasuchus.*

I wonder exactly how
cool they really were?

Upon investigating some interesting plants...
100%

...Kirrip's gizmo
unexpectedly pairs
with one of the seeds.

What the *what* now?

The thingamabob is operational!
WHIZZ
BLURP

and a gateway to the past opens.

Kirrip sets her status to 'Professor Kirrip is out of the office right now and will return in several million years.'

Behold, the Pleistocene!
Volcanoes. Lava. Rush-hour megafauna traffic.
Should have brought some sunscreen,
factor one-thousand.

On the plus side, that looks like a *Koolasuchus* fossil. ‘It seems they’re long gone by this time,’ says Kirrip. ‘I’ll have to travel further back… right after fleeing from that inconvenient volcanic eruption.’

The problem with sheltering from volcanic activity in a cave is that you're probably not the first one to come up with the idea.
A marsupial lion! *Thylacoleo carnifex,* if I'm not mistaken.

My friends call me Leo.
My enemies generally don't have
a chance to call me anything.

Have you heard of *Koolasuchus?*
Amphibious, about four metres long,
big flat head,
fangs,
laid-back attitude?

‘How about you run me through your inventory,’ Kirrip suggests, ready to take notes using The Monotreme Method: quill (ample supply) and ink (trickier to source).

'With pleasure!' Leo says.
'Let's see ... I've eaten

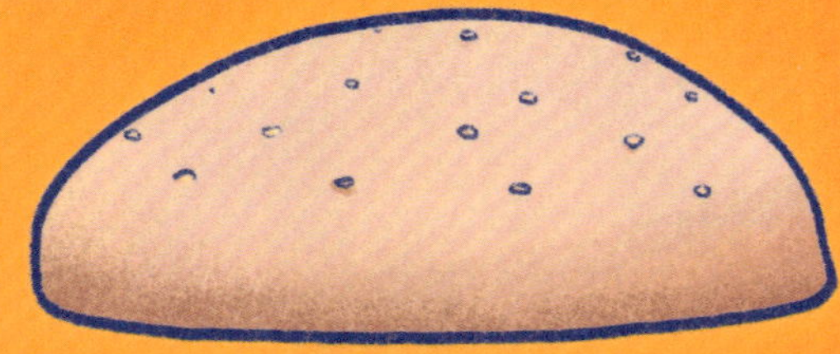

giant snakes,

giant kangaroos,

giant wombats,

Diprotodons

and the occasional *Genyornis.*

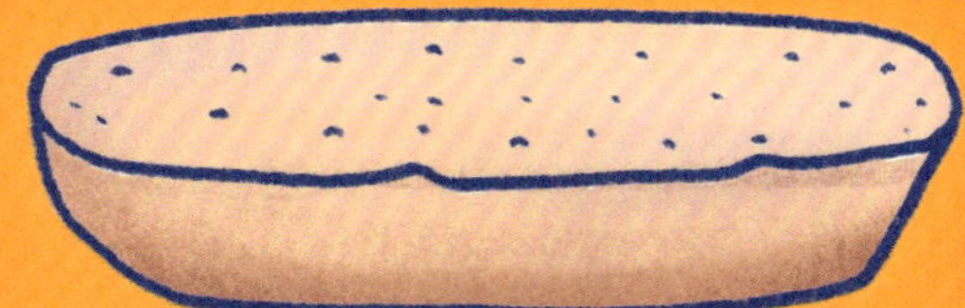

Bit feathery, those.'

Tell me, was *Koolasuchus* carnivorous?

They certainly were!
I hate to be rude, but so am I,
and you may have noticed a distinct
lack of echidnas among my trophies...

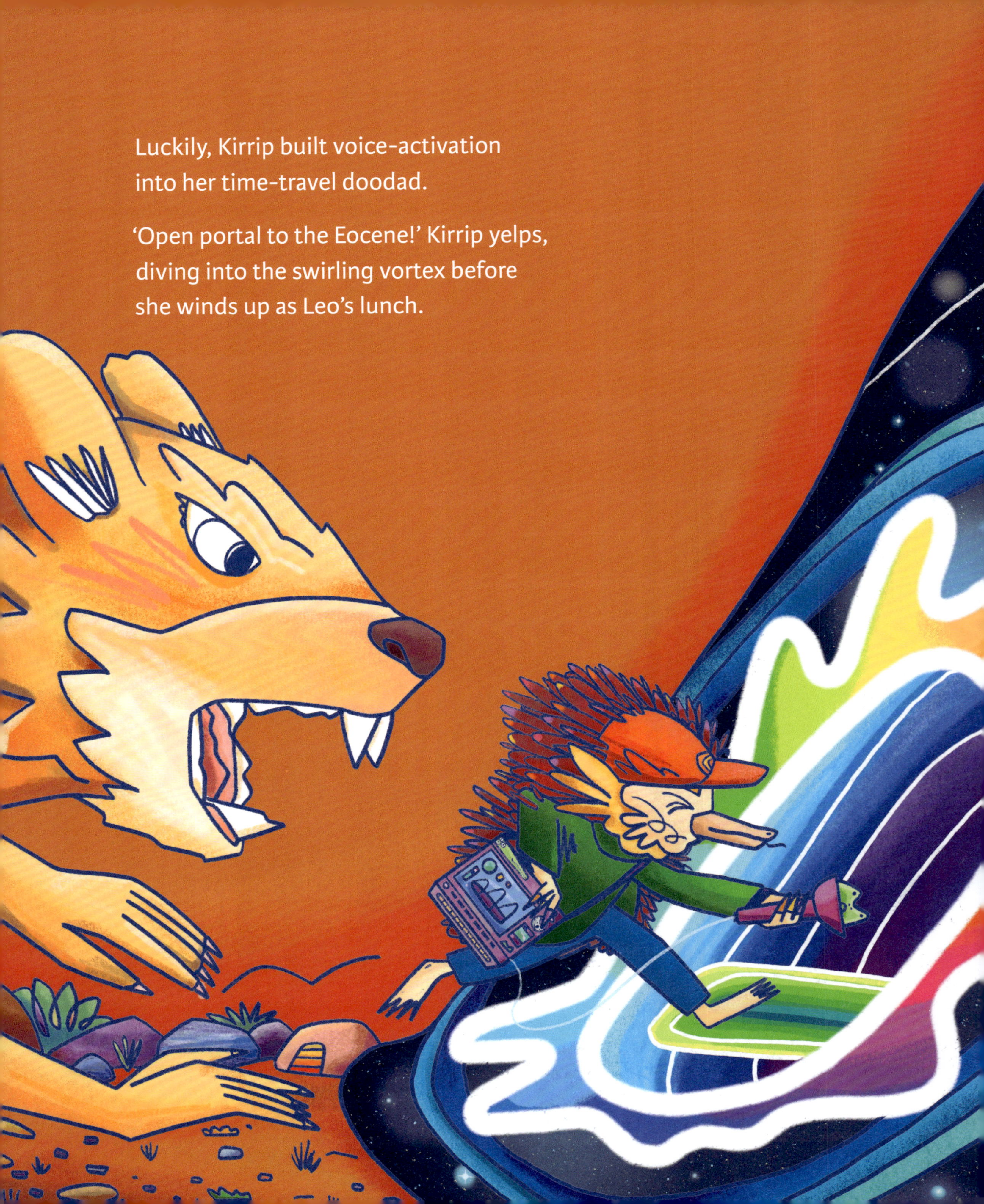

Luckily, Kirrip built voice-activation into her time-travel doodad.

'Open portal to the Eocene!' Kirrip yelps, diving into the swirling vortex before she winds up as Leo's lunch.

EOCENE *
MIL

Welcome to the Eocene.
Cliffs.
Beaches.
Awesome surf, dude.
Should've brought a boogie board.
There must be traces of *Koolasuchus* around here somewhere ...
EOCENE

'Can't a time-travelling echidna academic take a stroll on the beach to look for fossils in peace?' Kirrip grumbles, dangling from the talons of a *Pelagornis*.

Dropped into a nest,
Kirrip eyes the chicks warily.
Nice place you have here.
Coastal property is easier to find since we split from the Antarctic.
Great time to build a holiday nest!

Do you think she'd taste spicy?
Acidic, actually. You'd have awful indigestion.

Time for a sharp exit.

'Set coordinates for the Cretaceous!'
Kirrip tells her whatchamacallit.

CRETACEOUS
ZONE

Contemplate the Cretaceous!
So cool and leafy.

'This is more like it,' Kirrip says,
tracking the distinctive footprints
of *Koolasuchus* towards a nearby creek.

You know, you're pretty famous in my time.
Coolness never fades. More larvae, Professor?
A few for the road and then I'm off home. I have to get back to my lab—time waits for no monotreme!

CLUB

KOOL KLUES

Holocene *(11,700 to present day)*

Pleistocene *(2.58m – 11,700 years ago)*

SCIENTIFIC NAME:
Tachyglossus aculeatus

HOLOCENE

TYPE: Short-beaked echidna
Monotreme/mammal

SIZE: 40 to 55 centimetres long.
SPECIAL FEATURES: Sharp spines across its back. Short, slender snout. Sharp claws. Long tongue, perfect for scooping up ants, larvae and other snacks.

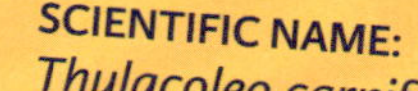

SCIENTIFIC NAME:
Thylacoleo carnifex

PLEISTOCENE

TYPE: Carnivorous marsupial lion

SIZE: 1.5 metres long, 100 to 150 kilograms.
SPECIAL FEATURES: Great climber. Powerful jaws. Semi-opposable thumbs with large, retractable claws.

Kirrip is a Woi Wurrung word meaning 'friend'. Woi Wurrung is the language of the Wurundjeri People.

Koolasuchus cleelandi is the official fossil emblem of Victoria.

The car-sized amphibian lived alongside dinosaurs during the Cretaceous Period. In a head the size of a wheelie-bin lid were dozens of ridged fangs for piercing prey, and two-inch tusks growing from the roof of its mouth.

Koolasuchus is unique to Victoria. Its fossils are only found at a few beaches and coves on Boonwurrung Country in South Gippsland. The Traditional Owners of this Land are the Bunurong People.

SCIENTIFIC NAME: *Koolasuchus cleelandi* — **CRETACEOUS**

TYPE: Carnivorous amphibian

SIZE: About 4 metres long.
SPECIAL FEATURES: Lived in fast-moving streams. Ate small dinosaurs, turtles and fish.

Eocene (56m – 33.9m years ago)

Cretaceous (145m – 66m years ago)

To learn more, visit the *Gandel Gondwana Garden* at Melbourne Museum.